Pretty Salma

Story and pictures by
Niki Daly

F
FRANCES LINCOLN
CHILDREN'S BOOKS

Salma lived with her granny and grandfather on the quiet side of town. One day, her granny said, "Salma! Pretty Salma, please go to market for your old granny who loves you so."

Salma put on her blue scarf,

her stripy *ntama*,

her pretty white beads

and her yellow sandals.

She tucked Granny's shopping list
in her ntama, lifted Granny's big
straw basket on to her head
and kissed Granny goodbye.
"Straight there and back again!"
said Granny. "And DON'T talk
to strangers, you hear!"
"OK, I promise," said Salma.

Off went Salma, *flip-flop*, *flip-flop* in her yellow
sandals. As she walked, she sang
her favourite song:

Oh, Salma, pretty Salma,
Come kiss Granny,
your darling old Granny
who loves you soooooo!

At the market
she bought
a giant watermelon,

a rooster with crazy eyes,

an ice-cold pink drink
and a bunch of
candy-striped straws.

The sun was growing hot and silly. The basket pressed down so hard on Salma's head that she forgot what to do next. So, instead of going straight home, she day-dreamed and dawdled into the wild side of town.

"Where are you going, little girl?"
asked a stranger.
It was Mr Dog.
Pretty Salma quite forgot that
she must not talk to strangers!
Instead, she talked and talked
until Mr Dog knew all about her
and her old granny.

"Your basket is much too heavy for
such a pretty little head," said Mr Dog.
"Allow me to carry it home for you."
Salma did feel a bit dizzy, so she agreed
to let Mr Dog carry her basket.
"I'm really looking forward to meeting
your granny," said Mr Dog.

After a while, Mr Dog asked,
"What are you wearing on your feet?"
"Sandals," replied Pretty Salma.
"Well, I should love to see how
they fit *my* feet," he said.

So they stopped,
and Mr Dog slipped
his big feet into
Salma's sandals.

On they went, *floppety-flip, flippety-flop*!
After a while Mr Dog asked, "What's that wrap
you're wearing?"
"My ntama," replied Salma.
"Mmm, I bet I'd look pretty in your ntama,"
said Mr Dog.

No sooner had Mr Dog wrapped
Salma's ntama around himself than
he asked for her scarf and pretty beads.
"How do I look?" asked Mr Dog,
striking a pose.
"Um, you look…

... *silly!*" thought Salma, running after Mr Dog as he strutted off.
Salma began to miss her things. But when she asked for them back,
Mr Dog said, "You'll get them back as soon as you teach me to sing."
So Salma tried to teach him her favourite song:

> *Oh, Salma, pretty Salma,*
> *Come kiss Granny,*
> *your darling old Granny*
> *who loves you sooooooo!*

But Mr Dog was hopeless at singing.
All he could do was go

WOOF!

WOOF!

WOOF!

"I need a *lot* more practice before I can sing," said Mr Dog,
"and until I learn to sing, you won't get your things back!"

Salma begged, Salma pleaded, "Mr Dog, Mr Dog,
please give me back my things!"
Mr Dog growled, "Sssh! You will never,
ever get your things back!
Now run away, little girl,
before I bite you
in two!"

Poor Salma got such a fright when she saw his sharp teeth
that she ran… and ran… and ran…

until she found her grandfather, telling stories,
dressed in his Anansi costume.

When Grandfather heard Salma's story, he said, "That's a very exciting story, Salma, but it doesn't sound like a happy ending. How can we save Granny?"

"I know," said Salma.
"We'll scare Mr Dog!"
"Exactly *how* will we scare Mr Dog?" asked Grandfather.
"Like this!" said Salma, putting on the mask of Ka Ka Motobi the Bogeyman.

Salma picked up Anansi's *atumpan* and beat it loudly,
Goema goema! Grandfather picked up his rattles
and gave them a fierce shake, *Shooka shooka!*
Little Abubaker, who loved
a good story, joined in with
clapping sticks, *Kattack-attack!*
"Let's go!" cried Salma.

Meanwhile...

…when Granny, whose eyesight wasn't too good,
saw Mr Dog flip-flopping up the path,
she thought it was her pretty Salma.
"Salma, Pretty Salma, come give
your granny who loves you a kiss!"
cried Granny. Mr Dog leapt up
and gave her a sloppy kiss.
"Oh my, Salma," said Granny.
"What a wet nose you have!"

Granny took the heavy basket from Mr Dog
and said, "Salma, Pretty Salma, you look hungry.
Let's eat!" Mr Dog started to chase the
crazy-eyed rooster round and round.
"Oh my, Salma," said Granny.
"What an appetite you have!"

Then Granny said, "Salma, Pretty Salma,
it's time for your bath."
Into the bath leapt Mr Dog.
"Oh my, Salma," said Granny.
"What hairy ears you have!
Are you sure you are my Pretty Salma?"
"Oh, yes, yes, yes!" cried Mr Dog,
jumping on to Granny's lap
and wagging his tail.
Now Granny was really worried!
Did her Pretty Salma have a tail?
Perhaps this wasn't her Pretty Salma!

Well, there was only one way to find out –
"Let's sing our favourite song," said
Granny, and she started to sing,

"Oh, Salma, pretty Salma!
Come kiss Granny,
Your darling old Granny
who loves you soooooooo!"

"WOOF! WOOF! WOOF!"
barked Mr Dog.
Then Granny knew she had been tricked.

She reached for her broom. "Out! Get out!"
But Mr Dog liked being Pretty Salma far too much
to leave Granny's house, so instead he growled
and snapped at her.

Granny was afraid Mr Dog would bite her in two,
so she jumped into her cooking pot. Mr Dog pushed
the lid down. *"Mmm… nice,"* he thought, *"Granny soup!"*
Granny cried,

"Help, help, help!"

Just then, the door burst open with a loud

Goema goema!
Shooka shooka!
Kattack–attack!

When Mr Dog saw Ka Ka Motobi the Bogeyman
and his gang, he got a terrible fright.

That bad dog slipped and tripped over
his miserable tail – right out of the house,
back to the wild side of town.

Salma took off her mask
and helped Granny climb
out of the pot.

Then they all sat down
to eat watermelon and
sip an ice-cold pink drink
through candy-striped straws.

The next day, Granny sent Salma to market to buy new clothes. Salma went straight there and back. And she never talked to strangers again!